For winged travelers
and those who ease their journey.

H.H.

For Mary, a special love
who always appreciated the beauty of ducks.

D.C.

Book Design by Cecile Birchler

Published by Ducks Unlimited, Inc.
L. J. Mayeux, President
Julius Wall, Chairman of the Board
D. A. (Don) Young, Executive Vice President

ISBN: 1-57223-398-2
Published September 2000

Ducks Unlimited, Inc.
The mission of Ducks Unlimited is to fulfill the annual life cycle needs of North American waterfowl by protecting, enhancing, restoring, and managing important wetlands and associated uplands. Since its founding in 1937, DU has raised more than $1.3 billion, which has contributed to the conservation of over 9.4 million acres of prime wildlife habitat in all fifty states, each of the Canadian provinces, and in key areas of Mexico. In the U.S. alone, DU has helped to conserve over 2 million acres of waterfowl habitat. Some 900 species of wildlife live and flourish on DU projects, including many threatened and endangered species.

Hutchins, H. J. (Hazel J.)
   The wide world of Suzie Mallard/Hazel Hutchins; illustrated by Dominic Catalano
   p. cm.
   Summary: Follows the first year in the life of a duck that is born on the Canadian prairie, flies along the Mississippi River, is injured and cared for, before returning home.
   ISBN 1-57223-398-2 (alk. Paper)
Mallard-Juvenile fiction. [1. Mallard-Fiction. 2. Ducks-Fiction.] I. Catalano, Dominic, ill. II. Title.

PZ10.3.H9685 Wi 2000
[E]-dc21   00-064340

The
Wide World
of
Suzie
Mallard

The Wide World of Suzie Mallard

Hazel Hutchins

Illustrated by
Dominic Catalano

DUCKS UNLIMITED

T he first sound from
Suzie Mallard's world
is a clicking sound.

Mama rises on her orange legs,
looks down.
"Kuk, kuk," she talks to her eggs.

Another egg clicks.
Clicking first, then peeping.
"Come out, come out,"
the eggs call back and forth.
"TOGETHER! COME OUT!"

On the third day together
they break into the world.

It is spring on the prairies in Canada.

"HELLO, HELLO, HELLO!" in duck talk.
They know each other's voices.
They know their mama's voice.
They rest and dry and move around.
Soon they peck at moving things
To see if they are good to eat.

Mama calls them from the nest.
"Quack, quack, kuk, kuk, follow,
follow, follow."

Suzie follows with her nest mates
through grasses thick as forests
over hills as big as mountains.

SWIM!

With big webbed feet
they scoot and zip and dive.
They eat and eat and eat.
And still they talk among themselves
"Here, lost, here, together, come, here!"
and tuck themselves beneath
their mother's wing at night.

"HIDE!"
Mother's call is urgent on the air.

Suzie hides among the reeds
feels the panic
hears her mother's injured flapping
frantic awkward.

Close behind her a mink is hunting.
Almost, he grabs her.
Almost again.
Farther and farther across the marsh
and then with one last lunge he tastes...

...DEFEAT!

Mama Duck flies straight up
up and up unharmed
on strong, sure wings.
One of her best tricks perfectly completed.

"Come, come, come,"
she calls on the water.
All is safe and clear.

Weeks pass
ducklings grow
feathers grow.
Suzie grows more independent too and
more than mink have been watching.

TRAPPED!

Large hands hold her gently.
"Here, Steve, your first duck to band."

Smaller hands are more excited,
but careful still.
"I think this is the one that stands on that
flat rock and quacks at me."

A band is placed around her leg
crimped shut with pliers.
"May I help set her free?"

Now each day on the pond
Suzie and her nest mates flap their wings.

On windy days
their chests lift higher and higher
above the water.
One glorious day they are airborne.
AIRBORNE!
Who would have guessed they
could fly like this!
They swoop and dip and turn
and almost crash together as they land.

A little practice will make things perfect.
A little practice will take them
farther from home.

Days shorten.
Ducks gather.
Suzie is one of many now
that fly between the fields and
open water feeding restless.

Soon these lakes will freeze
and snow will blanket the grain.
No place for ducks.

The northern sky dawns clear
and full with the promise of wind.
That evening when the signal comes to fly
the flock lifts high and higher still
and does not stop.

Many wings
one wing
on and on they fly through dusk and darkness
to a place Suzie has not been before
but somehow knows.
A stopping place used by her
grandparents and great-grandparents
before her.

They rest and feed.

Two days later they fly again.
And again. And again.
Wind and wing and the world below
they are almost at their destination
when the storm hits
and knocks them cruelly from the sky.

On the floodplains
where the Mississippi River cuts a wide
swath through the forest
the food is rich and plentiful.
Flocks and flocks of water birds
swirl and spiral
feed and forage
swim and dabble.

And here Alicia finds Suzie Mallard
spent, exhausted
one wing injured.

"She must have come in during the storm
last night," says Grandpa.

Alicia takes young Suzie home
builds a pen beneath the live oak tree
brings her grain and water
talks Grandpa into doctoring her wing.

"Phone the number on her tag,"
says Grandpa.
"Perhaps we'll find out where she's from."

When they hear back
Alicia traces Suzie's journey on the map.
A thousand miles and many more
across half a continent.
No duck should have to fly so far!

But the world is wide and ever changing.
Day's lengthen, weather warms.
Suzie Mallard grows strong again.

Out on the floodplains
the ducks travel in pairs
restless, restless, restless.
With a stronger yearning too.
As they take flight they call to Suzie in her pen,
"Fly back to the northern nesting grounds."

The flocks have all left when the letter comes.
Hello from Canada.
I hear you rescued a duck I banded.
Thank you!
She'll come back here to nest, you know.
There's lots of water this year.

"She will not find her way
without the flock," says Alicia.
"Ducks know," replies Grandpa.
"It is too late in the season," she says.
"Summer days are long in the north,"
says Grandpa.
"I will miss her," Alicia says
and knows she has already set her free.

FLY!
By the sight of land and sun and stars
and a feeling in your wing no human
can divine
fly to the place that calls so strongly.

Three males
bright as newly minted pennies
come courting.
Suzie chooses the strongest, brightest,
boldest.

Now when she flies
her mate flies on her flank
When she stops to rest
he guards her jealously.

The very day Suzie and her mate arrive
Steve spots her.
What other banded duck would stand
on that flat rock and quack at him?
Almost he knows the spot she chooses
for her nest.
She lays one egg a day
while the male waits.
When the laying time is over
her mate departs.

Steve marks his calendar
28 days.
When the ducklings hatch—
yellow downies on the water—
he will write a letter to Alicia.

Suzie Mallard does not know about letters.
She does not care.
The world is wide but ducks have always
known the way.

She settles contentedly upon her eggs.

It will all start again
with a clicking sound.